The Chop

by

Graham Hurley

First published in 2008 in Great Britain by
Barrington Stoke Ltd
18 Walker Street, Edinburgh, EH3 7LP

www.barringtonstoke.co.uk

ISBN: 978-1-84299-555-6

Printed in Great Britain by Bell & Bain Ltd

A Note from the Author

All books come from one little seed. The seed for this book came from two sentences. What had made me write them? I saw them on the paper but I didn't know where they'd come from. Later on, a friend asked me if I was going to turn the sentences into a book. I only worked out then that I'd have to tell the story of Old Wonky, and his grandad, and the millions of deaths that came fluttering down on the wing ...

To Ben and Harry
with love and clifftops

With special thanks to our readers:

Brian Dobbie
Maria-Elena Heather
Barbara Kilpatrick
Sue McGeachin
David McIndoe
Nicola McManus
Beatrice Small

Contents

Chapter 1
Ring Tones

Dad died on Sunday. For now they've put him in the fridge at the supermarket because everywhere else is full. I'd like to go and see him and say good-bye but the supermarket's only open on Thursdays. Plus the supervisor put a padlock on the fridge because one of the lads from the check-outs came in to look for space for his dead sister. The new Prime Minister was on TV again last night pretending to be Winston Churchill. That's a pity, too. Dad loved Churchill. I only wish he could have seen it.

My best friend Maddie thinks all this is a bit of a joke. Not a joke exactly, more a business opportunity. She and her partner, Elmore, invent ring tones for mobiles. Last night she rang me up and told me about it. Then she sent me a ring tone for free. Maddie says that people only talk on the phone now, and not face to face. That means there's big money in anything to do with phones and ring tones.

While I was chatting to Maddie, Mum double-boiled the eggs she gets free from the supermarket. Maddie told me her latest ring tone comes from a recording Elmore made at a funeral he went to last week. The funeral was in a little village called Bassington. It was a funeral for six people all at once. Elmore thought being in the church was a bit like being in a funeral factory. But everyone's dying now and no one wants to come out and meet anyone else so I can see the point.

Elmore said that he and the two undertakers and the new vicar were the only people in the church. That's a shame because Elmore's got a terrible voice and I expect they had to sing hymns. Afterwards all four of them stood by the big grave and Elmore had to help with getting all the coffins in. One of the dead people was the old vicar and they had to lay him down in the grave the other way round to everyone else. Elmore says that you bury ordinary people with their feet to the East so when they rise they face God. I thought that might be nice for the old vicar, too, but Elmore thinks he has to face West so when he rises up all the people that went to his church can see him. That's OK, I suppose. People might like someone in charge, even when they're dead.

I played Maddie's new ring tone to my mum after tea. It's just a church bell going *bong* every three seconds. Mum said she'd be scared to death to answer a ring tone like that because when you hear the *bongs* it means someone's died. I laughed and said it was probably Maddie's sense of humour. Maddie told me she wants to market the ring tone at a special toll-rate. That's a joke too. Tolls are the sound that sad bells make. Mum didn't think that was funny, either.

Mum works at the supermarket, by the way, which is why she gets the free eggs. No one else will buy them. It's why she could queue-jump, too, and get Dad into the big fridge. The big fridges are where they used to keep the frozen chickens. They're all empty now – except for Dad.

I don't know how it is with you but round our way they're definitely running out of places to put all the dead people. You've got to be a bit careful because dying doesn't kill the bird flu virus. It's still in the air and on the person's body even when they're dead. Up at the top of the estate there's an old bit of car park where everyone did their Cycling Proficiency. They've parked two of those big freezer lorries there now. The lorries come from the local chicken factory. Not many people know that. Our next-door neighbour told me. And she said if you look really hard you can see the words "farm-fresh" under the new paint they've used.

Our neighbour's sister lived on the estate too. She worked at the chicken factory. That's how our neighbour knows all about the lorries. The sister turned out to be one of the first people to be frozen. That's no surprise really. The virus loved chickens so no wonder it got her. She spent six hours a day tearing their innards out. Our neighbour says her sister always said she was immune to the virus because of her work, but she got exactly the same runny nose and sore throat and everything that Dad got so it couldn't have been true, could it?

I was going to tell Mum about this, too, but in the end I didn't. At least Mum can sneak a look at Dad on Thursdays if she wants to. If he was up at the car park, that would be impossible. There's barbed wire, for one thing. And soldiers, with guns.

* * *

Thinking about guns, Mum says we're very lucky to be living in England just now. The virus is everywhere, of course – all over the world. And in some countries people have started to panic. There's lots of rioting when the vaccine starts getting short, and people ambushing lorries with fresh supplies. There's even fighting outside hospitals when people think there's loads of the vaccine inside.

Just yesterday on the TV news there was a film of the police shooting a man at a hospital in Paris. The man had taken a nurse hostage so that she'd inject him with the anti-virus vaccine. I don't think the police killed him, and Mum said a hospital was probably the best place to get shot in because he got treated right away.

Even so, all this violence is starting to make people frightened. You can see it in their faces if they're brave enough to go out. The police are frightened as well. You always see policemen in twos and threes these days and they all carry guns, too, but we're not very keen on rioting in England so it's still pretty safe. Like Dad said, it's the virus that'll get you, not a bullet.

Chapter 2
Dad

About Dad. The funny thing is, he'd been old ever since I can remember, much older than Mum. Mum's still very beautiful, even at 50. It was her birthday a few weeks ago, and when I last did the sums I worked out that she was only fifteen when she had me. That made Dad twice as old as her. Part of the shame of him dying was all the pension he missed. In between listening to his Churchill tapes and reading about the Battle of Britain, he'd been looking forward to getting out a bit more. He'd wanted to take Mum to Paris on the train but Paris is closed, too, just like London. At least that's what Dad told me. He was already sneezing by then. Now I know that's not a good sign, so maybe he got the Paris bit wrong. It wouldn't have made any difference, I thought. If you've got a cold, you're not allowed to buy a ticket at the station, even with a vaccination certificate, and Mum hates walking, especially as far as Paris.

It's funny not having Dad at home any more. He didn't ever talk much, not that I can remember, but Mum thought the world of him. When I was a kid, Dad used to keep pigs. Our grandad, Mum's dad, worked on a farm all his life and Mum says he was always trying to teach Dad about horses and fields and hedges and stuff but Dad never wanted to know. He said he never wanted to work for a big farmer because that way they owned you, a bit like you were one of their animals. Better to set up by yourself, just a little bit of land and a few pigs. That's what he did.

He started with a kind of pig called a hybrid, that's a pig made with lots of other kinds of pigs. Then, when the babies came along, they got fat very quickly and in the end they went off to become sausages and streaky bacon. Dad used to get very upset about all this because you can get to be good friends with pigs. He hated seeing them going off to the sausage factory. In the end Mum said he'd be better off thinking about chickens, rather than pigs, because then he might start talking to her, rather than to the pigs, but Dad never had any time for chickens. He thought they were stupid and smelly and boring and he wouldn't even eat them on Sundays when they got really cheap. That upset Mum, too, because we never had much money.

* * *

Our town is called Overly. Before the virus started, everyone used to go on and on about the terrible traffic jams. I work as the lollipop man outside the school, helping all the kids and mums across the road. I've been doing it for nearly 20 years now and it's true that the queues of cars were getting longer and longer before the virus. The little ones who've just started school are really slow, even with their mums, and sometimes the drivers would get angry, especially the men. But now there's the virus, the roads are empty. They closed the school weeks ago, after one of the dinner ladies got sick and died. I still turn up for work every day, just in case. They might forget to tell me if the school was open again and then there'd be no lollipop man. You can never be too careful, especially these days.

I've always lived at home, mostly because I've never wanted to leave. Mum and Dad gave me the little bedroom at the back. I've got some of Dad's Airfix wartime plastic aeroplanes he used to make hanging on bits of string, and when the wind's blowing from the East they all move around in the breeze from the window. If I wake up in the winter and hear the Spitfires and German planes banging together over my head I know it's going to be really cold. On those days I wear a big thick pullover under my yellow coat and I borrow a pair of Dad's old gloves because that's better for holding the metal pole on the lollipop. I've got boots, too, with fleecy insides, but they make pedalling my tricycle a bit difficult.

My tricycle's a Pashley Picador with three gears and a big metal basket on the back. The basket's really useful now because I've started getting shopping for all sorts of people on Thursdays when the supermarket's open. The supermarket's at the bottom of the hill by the station, which means lots of pedalling back to the estate with a full load, and Mum says I'm losing tons of weight.

One of the last things Dad did before he got sick was to fix a metal stick onto the back of my trike. Elmore and Maddie are always going to Tibet and last time they went they brought me back some prayer flags. The flags are like long banners. They come in all colours, like yellow, green and red, and Maddie wrote me out what each flag means. The Tibetans all live in the mountains and they believe the wind is good for us and makes things better for everyone. There's lots of wind in the mountains. They make prayer flags that flap in the wind.

I've got lots of flags which I tie to Dad's pole on the back of the trike, and each day I change them around. I've got a Large Wind Horse Flag, and an Extra Power Flag, but my favourite is the Big Luck Flag. It's got a peacock on it, and an elephant and a wind horse, and it's meant to protect life and health.

I'm telling you all this because it says on the news that the people in Tibet don't get the virus much. That must have a lot to do with the prayer flags they fly. I've tried telling other people about this, and I've even said I'll lend them a flag or two to try it out for themselves, but they don't seem very sure. They say this country's different from Tibet.

Maybe they've got a point. The morning Dad was especially ill I parked the trike under his window with the Big Luck Flag on the back but there wasn't much wind that day and he died just after lunch.

* * *

Dad going like that was very sad. Twice running I've tried to get the key to his fridge at the supermarket but the supervisor keeps saying no. He never says no to Mum but I think that's because he likes her a lot, especially now Dad's gone. Like I said earlier, it would be nice to say goodbye properly but I don't suppose Dad would even notice. But that's not the point, is it? You've only got one dad, and life's not the same now he's not here.

Dad's favourite model aircraft was a big black Lancaster bomber. He took weeks making it, and painting it and stuff, and then he hung it up in the bedroom where him and Mum sleep. I thought Mum would take it down right away. It's right over where she sits in front of her dressing table and you can't look at yourself in the mirror without seeing this huge black thing with the bomb-bay doors open but she doesn't seem to mind.

When I asked her why not she said about Grandad, and what he did in the war. Dad told me once about him being a tail gunner on the Lanc, stuck out at the back for hours on end in the freezing cold, way up in the sky over bits of Germany. He said I should ask Grandad about it myself, and I will. It turns out Mum really loves that model Lanc. After Dad died I tried to take it down, thinking it made her sad, but she wouldn't hear of it.

Chapter 3
The Chop

Grandad's real name is Arthur Blossom. He's very old, 84, and he's very little and very brown, even in winter. He's got very blue eyes that go watery when the weather's cold and he's also got quite a big nose that goes red round the nostrils when he has to blow it too much. He lives in a little cottage out Fetbury way and it takes me about half an hour to get there if I'm not having to go into the wind.

Grandad worked on farms all his life, because there wasn't much else to do, especially in the olden days. He's still got a patch of garden round the back of the cottage near where he keeps his pigeons and he's out there most days. In the summer, like now, he grows strawberries especially for Mum because he knows she loves them. I like them, too. I go out there a lot. I take him milk from a farm down the road, and stuff from the supermarket. Grandad calls me Old Wonky. I don't know why he calls me Old Wonky but I think it's got to do with the way I ride the trike.

* * *

Yesterday, I was asking Grandad what he thought about the flu virus and everything. He just laughed. He's got an old telly in the cottage which he watches a lot and we started talking about having to show vaccination certificates before you got to be with other people (like on trains or buses or in shops). Grandad told me you can get fake certificates now, sold by criminals, but they cost at least

£100, which is a lot of money on top of a bus fare.

Like me, Grandad thought that was quite funny. Then he said something else which made me think a bit. In World War I – that's the war Grandad's dad was in – seven million people got killed. Then, at the end of the war there was a special and very horrible kind of flu which Grandad thinks came from pigs and guess how many people caught the flu and died from *that?* One hundred *million.* That's more than all the people in England, which is a lot.

Whenever I go over to Grandad's cottage he takes me round the back to see his pigeons. He used to race these pigeons in proper pigeon races but it got too expensive so now he just lets them out for a fly on Tuesdays, Thursdays and Sundays. Yesterday was a Thursday and they all went out for a fly but only four came back (out of nineteen). Grandad says he heard a gun being fired while the pigeons were out so he's been on the phone to the farmer to find out what happened.

The farmer's name is Mr Jenkins and he shoots birds a lot. In fact I used to help Mr Jenkins when he had pheasants. That was when rich people came down from London to shoot them. Mr Jenkins *said* he didn't know anything about the pigeons but the way Grandad told me I know he doesn't believe him. People hate all birds now, because of the flu virus, but Grandad really loves those pigeons of his and I saw how upset he was. Everyone knows they're his pigeons because of the way they fly together, round and round, and killing them, Grandad said, is like if someone aimed a gun at him.

Grandad used to work for Mr Jenkins' dad before he died (not of the flu), and Grandad's cottage still belongs to the farm. Grandad isn't very happy about that, either, especially because he once tried to buy the cottage but Jenkins just laughed and said he'd never be able to afford it. Grandad still says that was rude and ignorant.

When money was different Grandad says he only ever spent coins and never notes. He put all the pound and ten shilling notes in Branston Pickle jars in the cupboard where he still keeps his own shotgun and by the time he wanted to buy the cottage he'd started his seventh jar. A while back, Grandad twisted his ankle because he fell over a molehill in the dark and Mum said he could come and live with us. And she meant not just until his ankle got better but forever. Grandad said no. He said he'd seen what happened when old people got hidden away in their own families and he never wanted that to happen to him. The only person to carry him out of his cottage would be the undertaker and until that happened, thank you very much, he'd look after himself. Grandad is like that, very stubborn. Maybe that's why I like him so much. He knows who he is. A bit like me.

Thinking of Mr Jenkins and the pigeons made me ask Grandad about his time in the Lancaster bomber. Grandad has always been a good shot – that must have come from being in the war. Dad showed me a photo once of Grandad in his little glass turret at the back of the bomber plane. The plane looked huge. The turret went round and round and Grandad had four guns, two on one side, two on the other. Grandad's job was to shoot German planes before they shot him.

In the photo Grandad is grinning fit to bust and when I asked him why, he said the photographer had brought his girlfriend along to show her the aeroplanes. Grandad says she was really pretty and when he blew her a kiss she winked back. They went bombing that night and nearly crashed on the way home, which Grandad said would have been a shame. The girl's name was Frances. I think Grandad must have seen quite a lot of her afterwards because in the end they got married and soon after that Frances had my mum and her name's Peggy. Grandad said flying in bombers the way he did was dangerous. Lots of people he knew in other planes never came back. They got shot down by the Germans or crashed for some other reason and if you crashed you mostly got killed. They called that The Chop. You never knew when it was going to happen and you never thought it would happen to you but the more you flew, and the more that people you knew didn't come back, the more you started to think about The Chop.

There was a special look people had when they got frightened about The Chop. Grandad and his friends called it the Chop Look. They went all silent or they laughed too loudly at silly jokes or they stopped eating and got a bit pale. Funny. I've seen a lot of people round town like that this week. Maybe they're thinking about The Chop, too.

I asked Grandad why he wanted to be in the war when it was so dangerous and he said you didn't have much of a choice. You could go in the army or the navy or the air force. He didn't want to be a soldier because that's what his dad had been, in the war before, and it was horrible. He didn't want to be in the navy, either, because he gets seasick, even on the boating lake at Great Yarmouth. So that left the air force.

The other thing about the air force was you got really good food, like eggs and bacon, before you went off to drop bombs on the Germans. The other thing was that some of the Lancaster bomber airfields were round our way so he could get home when there was time between ops. Ops is short for operations which was the name for when you flew off to Germany. Eggs and bacon, by the way, is my big favourite, as well.

Grandad flew in his Lancasters from an airfield which is near us. The airfield was built specially for the war but Grandad said it wasn't up to much. All the flyers lived together in huts. By the time Grandad got there it was the middle of winter and there were no cupboards or chairs or tables – only bunk beds. When Grandad asked why, they said it was because they'd had to burn it all on the hut stove to keep warm.

The first thing Grandad told me about the turret at the back of the Lancaster was how cold it was. He called it his castle. He had to wear all kinds of special clothes and even then he was still freezing. That must be why Grandad has the fire going in the cottage all the time. He still chops the wood himself so he must still be very strong.

When I asked Grandad about dropping the bombs he showed me some photos from a book he's got. The photos are all black and white. Someone took those photos from way up in the Lanc – that's the Lancaster bomber – but you can still see the explosions on the ground. They look like fireworks, or maybe little white flowers in the dark.

Grandad's job was to look for German fighter planes out in the night sky but even when he saw them first, he never fired his guns until they fired theirs in case they hadn't seen him. When they fired he said it was like a string of little sausages coming towards you. He called it "tracer", and if one hit you, you probably got The Chop.

I told Grandad how Dad liked Churchill's speeches but it turns out Grandad's got no time for Churchill. After Grandad had won the war, and the fighting and the bombing was over, Churchill made another big speech on the radio. He went through thanking everyone – all the soldiers, and sailors, and fighter pilots, and everyone – but he never said a word about Grandad's lot. They were called Bomber Command. They were very fed up Churchill didn't thank them because half of them had died trying to drop all those bombs. Grandad said he and a few others had half a mind to jump in a Lanc and drop a couple more bombs on Churchill himself, just to show him.

There must have been funny times, as well, during the war, and Grandad says there were. Some nights, if they weren't going bombing, they went to the pub instead. It was called The Bull. It was a few miles from the airfield so they used to go there by bike. One night, after they'd just done 30 ops, they got really drunk and came back in the dark in formation on their bikes. Formation is how the planes flew together when they went off to Germany. On the way home that night Grandad fell off his bike and ended up in a ditch and he went to sleep there. He got into trouble next day but he didn't really care because he'd just done 30 ops. After 30 ops, you got a long break before you went bombing again. It was nearly the end of the war by then and Grandad never flew again. Not even to bomb Churchill.

Chapter 4
Pigeons

When I got home yesterday after I'd been to see Grandad, Mum was with a woman I didn't know. She was rather old, maybe even older than Mum, and very tall and thin. Mum had met her at work, because it was Thursday and the supermarket was open, and she'd brought her home to meet me. Mum knew I'd be back from Grandad's in time for tea.

The woman's name was Dot. She came from Africa, a country called Zimbabwe (which she called "Zim"). She'd been there all her life on a farm with her husband, and he was still out there looking after things. There was all kinds of trouble in Zim so Dot had come to work in England. She had a job in a big manor house out beyond Fetbury looking after a very old lady who had lots of money but wasn't very well. Dot said she did everything for this old lady, who spent most of her time in bed. She had to be with her most of the time. The supermarket used to deliver all the food and stuff but it wouldn't do that any more. She'd said all this to Mum and Mum thought of me. Maybe I could take stuff up to the manor house every Thursday?

When she said this, Dot looked at me with that special kind of smile people use when they really want a favour. She said she was worried about the old lady and the virus. I said of course I'd bring out her food and stuff. If she wanted me to, I could leave them out by the gate. She thought that was a terrific idea. She left some money with Mum and a list of stuff for next week. I looked at the list of shopping

after she'd gone. Someone in that house loved
Munchy Morsels but I didn't know what
Munchy Morsels were.

* * *

Two days later the phone rang. It was
Grandad. He wanted to talk to Mum. After
he'd finished, Mum said he was really upset
and told me to get over there as soon as I
could. When I asked what the matter was with
Grandad, she said it was to do with his pigeons.

Grandad was sitting in the cottage in his
pyjamas. For once, he didn't have the fire
going. In front of the fireplace were loads of
sheets of old newspaper. On top of the
newspaper, all floppy and dead, were his
pigeons. I counted them. There were fifteen.
He'd found them first thing in the morning.
Someone had wrapped them in the newspaper
and left them outside his gate. When I asked
who, he said Jenkins. Grandad heard the sound
of his Land Rover early in the morning. It had
a squeak from a wonky wheel. Jenkins' squeak.

I made Grandad some tea but he didn't drink it. He liked porridge in the mornings but he said he wasn't hungry. He just sat in his chair and stared at the dead pigeons. These days, you weren't supposed to be that close to birds. Dead birds carry the virus. I thought I should tell Grandad about that. I didn't. What was the point? There were little bloody marks on each of the pigeons where the shots had gone in so it couldn't have been bird flu because the virus kills from the inside. Grandad said it was murder. Jenkins had killed his pigeons. Given them The Chop.

I was going to tidy up the mess but Grandad said to leave them. He'd bury them later in the garden at the back. What mattered now was Mr Jenkins. Mr Jenkins knew what the pigeons had meant to Grandad. Why had he killed them?

Grandad is little but he has big, bony hands. Just then, he was tying his fingers in knots. Mum was right. He was really upset.

When I tried to cheer him up he didn't really listen. In the end I put the radio on. The man on the news was saying about how the government was planning to offer everyone counselling once the virus had gone. There'd be thousands of counsellors, enough for everyone. I could see Grandad was listening hard. When the man had finished, Grandad shook his head. He said the country he'd fought for – I think he meant bombed for – had gone. Now there were just sixty million people scared witless by a bunch of chickens. That was exactly what he said, except there was a rude word in there too, just before "chickens". When Grandad talks like this it means trouble.

Chapter 5
Burial

I didn't really know what to do so I went home. I went on Facebook. Maddie said she and Elmore had been trying to sell their new ring tones but no one wanted to buy them. I could have told her that already. That tolling bell is horrible, but Maddie never listens to me, so it wouldn't have made any difference.

Instead of ring tones, Elmore's got a new idea. People are getting very nervous about bird poo. If it gets on their cars, or their windows, or on bits of their gardens, they think it's full of the flu virus which is probably true. So what Elmore's made is a special scraper that's connected to a big tank of stuff with disinfectant in, in the back of their old camper van. They've both got bio-suits from the Red Cross lady in town and Elmore's got himself a special mask called the Advantage 3000.

Maddie says it's the ultimate in bird flu protection. It's got a full face cover and gives 100% visibility, and is made from a ballistic hard polycarbon. I think she got those last bits from the catalogue, because she never talks like that in real life. She also sent a photo of them both in their new uniform, ready to tackle splats of bird poo. She said they charge £106 a visit. I showed Mum the photo and she said Elmore and Maddie looked more frightening than the flu itself and that set me thinking. What does bird flu look like?

There's a special number you can phone. They give it out on TV. It's called the Flu Hotline. You ring it up and a computer voice asks you all kinds of questions. Do you want information about vaccinations, or medicines, or are you worried about getting to work? Have you just come back from a country with lots of flu in it? You have to press different buttons for different questions. I rang the Flu Hotline to ask what bird flu looked like but there was nothing about that. At the end of the message another voice said that there was going to be a Step Change. I didn't have a clue what he meant so I gave the phone to Mum but the voice had gone.

Mum said to turn on the TV. We went to BBC News 24. The man on the phone was right. We're now in something called Step Six, which sounds serious. It means no more football matches, no more cinema and plays, no more pubs, plus you have to have a special certificate if you want to be anywhere else with more than two people. The hospitals are all full now so they're going to put sick people in some of the empty schools. I was still thinking about whether they'd still need me as a lollipop man when Mum said about a website they gave out at the end of the news.

I went upstairs and put in the website address. It was something called UK Resilience. It said to enter a post-code. That took me to the East Suffolk Local Resilience Forum. It's all a bit tricky but it looks like Mum and I and everyone else down the road are either Stake-holders or Class One Responders. There was lots of stuff about vaccine uptake data and deaths projections but when I tried to find out about what the virus looks like, it basically said we should all sit tight and do nothing.

Mum and I were still thinking about this when the phone went. It was Maddie. She said Elmore had just found out that one of the people he helped bury the other day had been a Muslim. When Muslims are buried, they have to be pointed towards Mecca. The man Elmore buried hadn't been buried properly and some of his friends had found out. They were angry about it. Maddie sounded really worried about it. When I asked what was going to happen, she said Elmore had just gone out to dig the man up again. The friends had come round and when Elmore said he'd do it later because it was raining they hadn't been happy at all. I feel very sorry for Elmore. He hates the rain.

In the sitting room, the TV was still on. There's a man in charge of the flu in London but he's just been taken to hospital because he's got ill too. A doctor on the telly said this was really serious. The Flu Chief was only vaccinated weeks ago and that means the flu virus vaccine doesn't work properly any more. The doctor said the virus is always changing shape. It's as if it knows we're after it and keeps changing to hide from us. Clever.

* * *

Maddie's rung again. Tea time. She said that Elmore hasn't come home. He's been gone since this morning and she doesn't know why he's still not back. How can it take that long to dig someone up? She sounded worried so I said I could cycle over if it would help. She said yes so I tied on a special prayer flag for good luck (a red Wind Horse) and off I went. By the time I got there (against the wind), Elmore had turned up. There were loads of people with him and they had the dead man in the back of a van. They wanted to wash the body and Elmore was trying to find a bucket and a scrubbing brush.

The body was propped up in the van by some big sacks full of rice and a wooden tray loaded with those really big plastic tubs of hot pickle (not Branston).

The dead man had been a great footballer and his friends wanted to bury him in the corner of the football field where he'd scored loads of goals. Elmore wasn't very happy about this because the football field was miles away and he still had to fill in the grave in the

church yard at Bassington. In the end, he let
the friends borrow his spade and they
promised to bring it back as soon as they'd
finished. After they'd gone, Elmore had a bath.

Chapter 6
The Changes

The next Thursday, I went up to the supermarket with Dot's list for her and Mrs Bellamy. I thought at first that they'd run out of Munchy Morsels but then I saw that all the shelves were in a muddle and the Munchies, which are cat food, had got onto the jams shelf. I got ten tins of Munchy Morsels to be safe and all the other stuff Dot asked for. She wanted six cans of beer called Warka. I'd never heard of Warka before!

After the government saying about Step Six, and the Flu Chief dying, the supermarket was nearly empty. There was only one check-out working and the girl's nose was all red so no one except me went near her.

Her name's Kate. She's nice. I sometimes see her walking home when I'm on lollipop duty but I've always been too shy to say anything. In the supermarket, though, it seemed rude not to chat a bit because it must be terrible having everyone avoid you all the time. Kate told me that Warka beer comes from Poland. I asked her why Dot from Zimbabwe wanted to drink Polish beer but she said she hadn't got a clue. She doesn't know Dot and she's never heard of Zimbabwe. Maybe I should have talked about something else.

After the supermarket, on the way to deliver Dot's shopping, I suddenly heard the sound of church bells. It was very soft to begin with but then it got louder and louder and pretty quickly I worked out it was coming from a little village called Kettlestead which is only a little way off the main road.

I know lots about church bells because of Grandad. He's been a bell-ringer all his life. In bell-ringing you ring Changes. Bell Changes are lots of different bells in different orders, and Grandad knows hundreds of them. He taught me some too, and did his best to make me a good bell-ringer. He used to take me to some of the churches and got me to hold the fluffy bit near the end of the big rope that dangles down from the church roof. That bit's called the Sally and it's a really good feeling when you pull the Sally and hear the bell go *bong* way up in the sky. There's more to it than that, of course, because you have to keep time with other people. If you want to know, I was never very good at it. But it didn't matter, though. I love bells.

After I heard the bells, I thought why not go to Kettlestead? The church is very old. I parked the trike under a tree in the grave-

yard. The big door at the end of the church
was open and I could hear people inside
grunting in time with the bells. It was dark
inside and it took me a time to see that one of
the men ringing the bells was Grandad. He
saw me come in and gave me a wink and
carried on ringing. He must have been pulling
really hard because his face was really sweaty.
The Change they were ringing was called The
Weasel because it sounds like Pop Goes The
Weasel. I listened for a bit and then got on the
trike again. I could still hear the bells when I
got to Dot's. By then it was just the one bell,
the biggest. It's called the tenor bell and it's
the one Grandad always rings. If you want to
know what it sounds like you should listen to
Maddie's ring tone. *Bong ... Bong ... Bong.* Like
I said earlier, that's called tolling. These days
especially, it's scary and it makes me feel sad.

I was leaving Dot's shopping at the gate at
the end of her drive when I heard a car
coming. I thought at first it was Dot but it

turned out to be a man in jeans and a T-shirt.
He was very friendly. He didn't speak very
good English and he said his name was Ivan.
He looked young, younger than me. The first
thing he did was to find the Warka beer in the
shopping. That made me guess he was Polish.
He offered me one but I said no because I don't
like beer. When I asked which part of Poland
he came from he said nowhere. He wasn't
Polish at all. He was Russian but liked Warka
because he'd been in Poland once and drunk a
lot.

He said he worked in a factory where they
pack loads of stuff for the supermarkets.
Before that he'd been sprout-picking in the
winter but he hated the job because it was so
cold. When I asked about Dot and Mrs Bellamy
he said that Mrs Bellamy was very old and
spent all her time in bed and never came
downstairs.

Dot was his real friend. He'd met her in
town. He'd been living in a terrible place and

Dot had told him about Mrs Bellamy. She'd said she needed someone to help with the old lady in the evenings. It was hard to do everything by herself. So, in the end, Ivan got all his things and came to Mrs Bellamy's house to live. He lived in a barn next to the farmhouse. The barn was made of really old wood. Ivan said the barn was full of rats and mice and little birds. He said that sometimes it was like living in a zoo.

* * *

When I got back home, Mum was looking especially happy. The supervisor from the supermarket had asked her out but in the end she'd said no because these days there's nowhere to go. She pulled a bit of a face when she said this because she's getting a bit fed up with so many people dying all the time. We watched the news together after tea. They might have to start closing some of the power stations because it's dangerous just to have skeleton staffs. *Skeleton* staffs? What does that mean?

Chapter 7
Chopped

Next day was a special day. That was when everything started to go wrong. The first thing that happened was a phone call from Grandad. He sounded out of breath. He said he needed a bit of help but wouldn't say why. Mum was going to have a word but he rang off. I got on my trike.

When I got to his cottage, the door was locked. I went round the back, looking in the windows, but I couldn't see him. I was wondering about getting a ladder and climbing up to his bedroom window when my mobile went off. It was Grandad. He must have been watching me. He was hiding in the bit of wood up behind the cottage.

There were loads of brambles and nettles and everything in that wood and I was stung all over by the time I found him. He'd made a little house for himself under a bush. He had some blankets, and a stove, and bread and milk and tea. He's got a big tarpaulin that he uses to keep the chopped logs dry and he'd dragged that up into the wood too. To begin with, I thought he'd gone potty, the way that old people do, but when I asked he said he'd never felt less potty in his life. Just then I saw the shotgun. It was half-hidden under the tarpaulin.

"Jenkins is a goner," he said. "And about time too."

Last night Grandad had been out with the gun, looking for rabbits. He was in another wood, about a mile from the cottage, when two pheasants flew over. Grandad loves pheasant but he was slow getting the gun up and anyway the light wasn't very good so he didn't even pull the trigger. A couple of seconds later he heard another gun, really close, bang-bang, both barrels. The pheasants both fell out of the sky. Grandad went into the wood because he thought he might get to the pheasants first. He didn't, but he did find Jenkins. Jenkins told Grandad he was trespassing.

Grandad didn't like the sound of that. He said the wood belonged to another farmer who didn't mind him being there. Jenkins just laughed. He said the other farmer had gone bust because of being a chicken farmer. All his chickens had had to be killed because of the virus. So then Jenkins had bought the wood off him for almost nothing. Jenkins said Grandad had to go away or else he'd call the police.

Grandad said he wasn't going anywhere until he got the truth about his pigeons. Had Jenkins been and shot them? Jenkins said yes, then he started laughing again which was a bit of a mistake because Grandad did the same to him.

Both barrels. Bang-bang. Chopped.

At first, I thought Grandad was joking but then he put his hand right under the tarpaulin and pulled out Jenkins' shot-gun. It was brand new. It must have cost loads.

"So where is he, Grandad?" I wanted to know.

"Still in the wood. Where I shot him," Grandad said.

"Is he dead?"

"Very. He was a big bloke, Jenkins." Grandad pointed to his own chest. "You couldn't miss."

"Why hasn't anyone been to look for him?" I asked.

"Maybe they have," Grandad said. "But I don't think so because he's been living alone since his wife went. I just thought you might help out."

"How?" I couldn't understand what Grandad wanted.

"We need to bury him. Get rid of him," Grandad said.

"When?" I asked.

"Tonight."

Friday nights I usually go to flower-arranging class with Mum. She loves flowers done a fancy way. But the classes have all stopped because of the virus.

Grandad said he had a spade. I rang Mum and said I was staying over at Grandad's. Once it got dark, Grandad and I'd go up to the wood and see about Jenkins. I was still thinking about the spade and the size of the hole we'd need when I had an idea. Grandad was watching me.

"Who are you phoning?" he asked me.

"A friend of mine. His name's Elmore," I said.

I asked Elmore about the Muslim he'd dug up at Bassington. Was the grave still open? Elmore said it was, because he and Maddie had been on three bird poo jobs and it had taken all day. I told him about Grandad, and about Jenkins, and he was a bit iffy at first but then I thought of Grandad's pickle jars – the ones he was going to use to buy the cottage – so I offered to pay him with some of the money Grandad had saved up. Then Elmore said he'd put Jenkins in with everyone else.

Elmore came over a couple of hours later with his camper van. We drove up to the wood. There was a track that went off the road and into the wood and Elmore was able to get quite close to where Grandad thought he'd killed Jenkins. It was quite spooky in the wood. All we could see was Grandad's torch. Grandad went on ahead to find the body. Then his torch went out and Grandad gave his owl hoot (which sounds really good) and me and Elmore got out of the van to help him.

Jenkins was really heavy, and quite slippery in places. We dragged him back to the van. Getting him into the van was hard because it was full of all Elmore's bird poo equipment but then Elmore came up with a brilliant idea.

The thing about Elmore is he reads lots of books, especially thrillers and crime stuff. He said we ought to cover our tracks and he had just the thing. He messed around in the back for a while and then got out with a bucket. He said it was full of this really powerful disinfectant. It would hide all the blood and stuff we'd left in the woods and no one would ever know. Elmore took Grandad's torch and walked off into the trees, the way we'd dragged Jenkins, splashing all this disinfectant around.

Grandad and I were still in the front of the van.

When Elmore got back, we drove off. Grandad was in the back. We had Jenkins hidden under a blanket, and Grandad was sitting on top. It's about ten miles from the wood to Bassington church where Elmore had dug up the Muslim. We were nearly there when Elmore said there was a police car behind us. It had the blue lights going and, after Elmore let it overtake, a sign came on in the back of the police car telling us to stop.

Two policemen got out. It was very dark. They both had torches. Elmore wound down his window. That time of night, they wanted to know what we were doing. Elmore said about the bird poo jobs, and how one had been really tricky, lots of big bird poo, really dangerous stuff, full of the virus. The policemen stepped back from the window. I nearly laughed out loud.

Then one policeman shone his torch in the back of the van and asked about Grandad. Elmore looked at me and I said Grandad had been at the last house we'd done and as a favour we were taking him to hospital because he kept sneezing and stuff. This was true. Grandad had been sneezing and coughing fit to bust.

The policeman wanted to know whether we had vaccination certificates. Elmore showed his but said it wasn't worth much because everyone knew the vaccines didn't work any more. The policeman gave him one of those long looks. Then he nodded, and took all our names and addresses, and said it was OK for us to carry on.

After the police car had gone, we got going again. We parked up by the church in Bassington and waited for at least an hour before getting out. It was very quiet around the church. It was a bit away from the village and there was a thick hedge around the grave-yard. When we had a look at the grave Elmore had opened, it was perfect. There were the five coffins at the bottom of the hole and plenty of room for Jenkins on top. We dragged him out of the van and dropped him in the hole. No one cared which way he faced, which I found a bit sad, but then we shovelled all the earth back in and trod on the top to get it flat.

We went back to Elmore's place that night because Grandad wasn't keen on sleeping at his cottage. The police had the address and as soon as someone called them about Jenkins going missing, they might come round to see what Grandad knew. Grandad said he needed to keep his head down for a while.

Elmore's place is very small so me and Grandad slept downstairs on the floor. Grandad snores a lot so I didn't get much sleep. That's as well as sneezing and then he began to wheeze. I got up at five o'clock and put the kettle on for tea. I thought about where else Grandad could hide. It was when I was looking for the sugar (which Grandad likes a lot) that I had my next brainwave.

Chapter 8
The Barn

I phoned Dot. Could she put Grandad up in the barn? She sounded a bit surprised to begin with, then said I should come over. I triked up to the farm. The old barn where Ivan lived was on the right-hand side before you got to the house. It was sagging in the middle, like someone had sat on it, but there were tiny windows in the side and Ivan (or maybe Dot) had put red curtains up. From the outside it looked quite cosy.

Dot met me outside the house. She wasn't wearing a mask and neither was I because it gets in the way on the trike, especially on hills or against the wind. When I asked again about Grandad, she put her hand on my arm.

"He's really your grandad?" she whispered.

"Yes," I said.

"And he's in some kind of trouble?" Dot went on.

"A bit," I said.

"No problem. You've been kind to me. These days, that matters."

She said that Grandad was welcome to move into the barn for a while. Maybe I could help sort things out. She had a spare bed in the house and a pair of pyjamas that had once belonged to Mrs Bellamy's husband. We carried the bed across to the barn and she went off to look for blankets and sheets and stuff.

The inside of the barn was brilliant. There were bales of hay up at one end and all kinds of old farm stuff hanging on the wall. I looked very hard but I couldn't see any rats or mice. Maybe they only came out at night.

Ivan lived at the other end of the barn. He'd hung sheets across to make a kind of wall. There was coconut matting on the floor, and a chest of drawers, and a table to eat from, and a pile of books in a funny language, and some shelves where he kept his clothes and his food. There were bits of candles on saucers everywhere and a couple of cats asleep on his bed. That's who all those tins of Munchy Morsels were for.

"So when can Grandad move in?" I asked.

* * *

Elmore drove Grandad over that same evening. I could tell Grandad loved the barn. Dot had made it really nice while I was gone and he had a whole bit to himself. He said he was a bit tired after helping bury Jenkins and he lay on his bed while I told him about Mum and the supervisor at the supermarket who was so keen on her, and it was nearly dark and I saw that Grandad was asleep.

It was true. There were *lots* of mice in that barn. If you really listened you could hear them up the other end, snuffling around in the hay. For a while I did my best to point the cats at them but all the Munchy Morsels had made the cats really lazy. It's the same with our cat at home. She gets one tin of cat food a day and after that she's always asleep.

Ivan came home from work just before I left. Grandad was still asleep. I think it was at this point that I thought something had gone wrong with Grandad's breathing. It was like he had bubbles in his throat. I didn't say anything because Grandad often got a bit of a chest but I know Ivan saw too because he said he'd keep an eye on him. That didn't seem fair. If Grandad was sick with the virus, why should I let Ivan get it too? Then I had another brainwave. Ivan could stay at Grandad's cottage!

I put this brainwave to Dot. Just in case there was something really wrong with Grandad, it would be better for Ivan not to be so close. She thought about it, then said she needed Ivan around to help in the house sometimes. I said I'd help her instead.

Dot agreed. She drove Ivan across to the cottage and when she came back I helped her with Mrs Bellamy. She was really old and lived in a huge bed in a big room with a lovely view from the window. She was a tiny woman with a nice smile and I helped Dot turn her in the bed and do some other things to make her comfortable.

Mrs Bellamy wore a little hat that Dot had knitted for her and I fed her barley soup from a little silver spoon. Mrs Bellamy had no teeth but she liked bread soaked in the soup. I wasn't very good with the spoon and soup kept spilling down her front but she didn't seem to mind. Dot made me an omelette afterwards and it took me until next day to ask where she'd got the eggs.

By then, Grandad had woken up. He seemed a bit better, but he said he had a pain in his chest. I made him some tea and Dot gave me half a loaf of bread that was still warm from the oven. She asked me about Grandad, and when I said about the pain in his chest and all the wheezing she gave me a funny look and said it was better if I didn't come in the house any more, just in case. I was going to ask how she'd get on with all the heavy jobs without me but I didn't get the chance because she'd run indoors.

I put butter on the bread and Grandad smiled when it went all gooey. He didn't eat very much of it but he said it tasted nice, like the proper bread he used to get in the olden days. I borrowed one of Ivan's chairs and sat by Grandad's bed all morning while he told me a bit more about the way things had been when he was young.

For instance, when he was little, they only had bread and jam and potatoes and swedes to eat. Then he started working in the fields as a stone picker for something called two shillings a day. After that he said he used to pull up dock weeds with his three sisters and later, when he was older, he used to take the cattle to market in Ipswich. Ipswich is nearly twenty miles from here, which is a long way, and then he had to walk back. All this time he didn't once talk about Jenkins and getting stopped by the police and getting rid of the body. I think he must have forgotten.

Chapter 9
Grandad's Secret

Much later that day Grandad started getting bad again. He said his throat was very sore and that he couldn't breathe properly. I thought about phoning the Flu Hot Line to check about whether he might have the virus but I hadn't got much credit left on my mobile and I knew I ought to ring Mum. I told her what had happened, and how Grandad was, and she sounded really worried. Mum said she'd come out first thing tomorrow and I must stay with Grandad.

That night, I started getting really worried. The wind was blowing stuff around in the yard and I went outside to where my trike was. I found the flag I keep specially for when things get bad. It's called The Victory Banner. It's got lots of writing on it and sometimes I think it's a bit muddly, but Maddie swears by it. She says the writing is to protect against really bad stuff. I tied the flag to the pole and put the trike out in the open where the wind was blowing hardest. Then I went back to Grandad and lit two more candles.

Grandad's breathing seemed a bit better. I sat on his bed and stroked his hand very softly so as not to wake him up but after a while he suddenly pushed back the blankets and got out of bed. I tried to stop him but he was really strong. He was trying to find his trousers. When I asked what the matter was he said the moles were back.

Ever since he broke his ankle, Grandad has always hated moles. They make tunnels under his little lawn in front of the cottage. One time he got a load of empty beer bottles and buried them with only the necks of the bottles showing, all pointing the same way. When I asked him why, he said they all pointed west to catch the wind, and when the wind blew, the bottles would make a special noise that would drive the moles crazy. Then all the moles would climb out of their tunnels and Grandad would do the rest. He has a big old stick and he chased them round the lawn with it. As soon as he'd found his trousers, he said, he was off to kill some more.

I got him back to bed. By now it was dark, and the wind was still blowing a gale, and I found myself a blanket and lay on the floor next to Grandad. I listened to the wind and I started to think about what it must like to be a mole, living underground with all the noise from those half-buried beer bottles driving you crazy. Then I thought about the prayer flags, and whether or not I'd tied on the right one, and then Grandad started to fidget again but this time he didn't get out of bed.

When I asked him how he felt, he said groggy. Groggy and very hot. I went outside to the yard. There was an outside tap and a bucket so I got some water. I found an old piece of towel that must have belonged to Ivan and dipped it in the water to wash Grandad's face. The water was very cold and seemed to make Grandad feel a bit better.

After a while he asked about the noise. I thought he meant all the scuffling from the mice and rats up the other end of the barn but then I saw I'd left the door to the yard open by mistake. What Grandad could hear was the snapping of the prayer flag in the wind. I got up to close the door but Grandad said to leave it. For a moment I thought he was going to tell me about the moles again but I think he'd forgotten about all that. All he wanted to listen to was the wind.

I sat on his bed for a long time, just holding his hand. He mumbled something about being Tail End Charlie and how a bad wind could wreck a landing. All this stuff was about the Lancaster and the war and I was going to say about Dad's plastic model bomber which was still in Mum's bedroom at home when Grandad gave my hand a big squeeze.

"You're a good boy," he wheezed.

I didn't know what to say. I squeezed his hand back. He was looking up at me. His eyes were all runny in the candlelight. I could see he was trying to tell me something else.

"I'm glad I had you," he said at last.

"Had me?" I asked.

"Yes." Another squeeze, softer this time. "Ask your Mum."

I stared at him. I didn't know what to say. I was a bit puzzled. *Had* me?

Grandad turned his head away so I couldn't see his face. He was trying to say something else but the words wouldn't come. I bent down very low and thought about mopping his face with the flannel again. Then he coughed for a bit and tried to sit up. I tried my best to help him. I could feel his bones under the pyjamas Dot had found for him.

"Beautiful." He was looking at me. "Kind, too."

"Who?" I asked.

"You, son." Grandad put his hand out to touch my face. "You ever think about that?"

"About what, Grandad?" I asked

"That ..." His fingers touched my nose.

I've got a very big nose, exactly like Grandad. I was about to ask him what he meant by calling me "son" but he started coughing again and then he lay back on the sheet and stared up at the roof of the barn. What was he seeing up there? When I looked, all I could make out was swallows' nests.

Grandad stayed like this for a long time. The wind got stronger and stronger outside and I could hear the prayer flag flapping away and I thought that was probably a good sign but after a few hours I saw Grandad had stopped breathing. I've never seen anyone die before, but it was a bit early to phone Mum.

* * *

The next thing I knew, she was standing next to the bed. She'd come over first thing to see how he was. I was lying beside him on the bed, sound asleep. Because it was still cold I'd covered him up with a blanket. She bent over and pulled the blanket away from his face. He looked very peaceful like that, much younger than he'd looked yesterday. She stared at him for a long time. I knew she wanted to cry and in the end she did.

When she'd dried her eyes, we went outside. It was Monday by now, and the prayer flag was just hanging from the pole on my trike because the wind had gone. Looking at it, I thought about what Grandad had said before he died. *Had* me?

"He said that?" Mum was staring at me.

"Yes."

"What else did he say?" she asked.

"He called me 'son'. Then he said we had the same noses ... and told me to ask you why."

Mum didn't say anything for a long time. Upstairs in the big house I could see Dot looking at us through a window. Then Mum put her arm through mine and we started walking down towards the road where she'd parked her car. There were rooks everywhere. I could hear them cawing.

"Grandad was right," Mum said at last. "He did have you."

I was frowning. "What do you mean?"
I asked her.

Mum gave me a look, then said it wasn't easy to explain. She said that after the war, Grandad's wife – Mum's mum, Frances – had died. That left Grandad and Mum living together in Grandad's cottage. Mum was fifteen and it was suddenly her job to look after Grandad.

"That must have been hard," I said.

"It was. And it was hard for Grandad, too," she told me.

"Of course." I was still watching the crows, trying to work it all out. "So was that why he found a girlfriend?"

I looked at Mum. She gave me a look back, quite a funny look, then squeezed my arm.

"Yes," she said.

"Was that girlfriend my real mum, then? Not you at all?" I couldn't work anything out now and I didn't like it. I like my mum to be my real mum. I always have.

"No." Mum was trying to be honest and nice at the same time. "It *was* me. I was Grandad's girlfriend for a bit. He gave me a baby. And that baby was you."

* * *

The rest of the day was very busy. Mum rang someone from the supermarket who came to pick up Grandad's body. The supervisor had found a space beside Dad in the supermarket freezer so now there were two reasons why I had to have a look in there. Mum said I could go in next Thursday. Then we went back home.

"If Grandad is my real dad, where does Dad come in?" I wanted to know.

Mum told me, "He was a man I met later, after you were born. He was older than me. He had a little pig farm over towards Stowmarket. Even Grandad liked him. He always loved you like a proper son. You can still think of him as your real dad if you want to."

I said I thought that might be easier. But I still couldn't stop thinking about Grandad.

"Why did he call me Old Wonky?" I asked Mum.

"Because he thought you had a screw loose," she said.

Someone else once told me this. At school. In the playground.

"And is that why I never passed any of those exams? Because I was called Old Wonky?"

"Yes. Sort of."

"And was that because of Grandad?"

"Yes ... and me. But we loved you a lot, and so did Dad. I promise," Mum said softly.

I knew it had to be serious.

"But do you still love me? Even if I'm a bit wonky?" I asked.

"Of course I do. Come here ..."

Mum's got a lovely hug but I think I gave up at that point. It was nice to be loved but I was in a bit of a muddle about dads. Also I was very sad about Grandad. I gave Elmore a ring. He'd just come back from taking Ivan across to Dot's place. He'd given the barn a real go with the disinfectant because we all knew Grandad had died of the virus but he'd told Dot that everything would be alright.

Elmore and Maddie are my best friends (apart from Mum) and I was going to tell him about Dad not being dad and Grandad being my real dad but then I had another idea.

"We ought to say a proper good-bye to Grandad." I told Elmore. "And I know just the way to do it."

* * *

We all met the next day at the little church on the edge of Bassington where we'd got rid of Jenkins. Elmore was there, and Maddie, and Ivan as well. I'd invited Dot but she had to be with Mrs Bellamy, and Mum was busy with the supervisor at the supermarket. Because I was the only one who knew how to do bell-ringing I had to explain the way it was done. We needed six people but the Prime Minister had just said that things had got even more serious – it was a State of Emergency – so I thought four would do.

The way you ring bells is to give the Sally a pull. This makes the bell in the roof turn right over and go *bong*. Every bell has a different *bong* and the simplest thing to do was to go from high to low with four bells.

Off we went. When you pull the Sally, the bell rope shoots up to the roof and it's important to hang onto the loop bit at the end. Elmore forgot and the rope shot up into the roof so it was all a bit of a mess to begin with. Maddie thought this was very funny and she was still laughing when she forgot about her rope, too, which made it even worse.

This was when the new vicar arrived. I explained about Grandad dying and how much he'd loved the bells. The vicar was very young. After I'd finished about Grandad, he went off to find his wife. It turned out that she was a real bell-ringer, not like us, and when they both came back we had six people – the right number to ring the bells properly. It took quite a long time but in the end it must have sounded OK because Dot rang Ivan on his mobile. She could hear the bells from miles away. Even Mrs Bellamy thought they sounded nice! That made me very pleased. Grandad would have been proud of us.

A bit later, we stopped. Everyone was quite tired because bell-ringing can be hard work but I was really sweating. When we went out into the fresh air I started shivering. The vicar's wife asked if I felt OK. I could see Elmore looking at me but I said I was fine, just a bit wonky.

Then I felt a sneeze coming, and I sniffed and I sniffed but there was nothing I could do to stop it.

Want More? Why not try these?

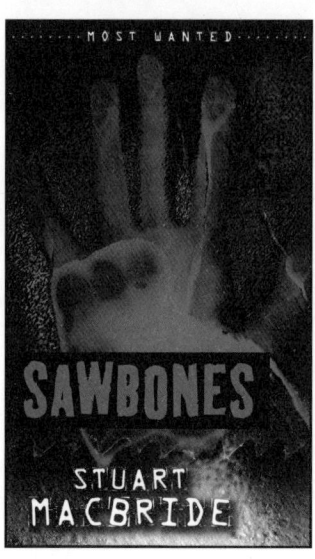

Sawbones
by
Stuart MacBride

They call him Sawbones: a serial killer touring America kidnapping young women. The latest victim is Laura Jones – the daughter of one of New York's biggest gangsters. Laura's dad wants revenge – and he knows just the guys to get it. Sawbones has picked on the wrong family ...

Dead Brigade
by
James Lovegrove

A new kind of solider ... This is the British Army of the future. Soldiers brought back from the dead to fight as robots. The zombie army can learn. They can kill. The only thing they can't do is die. Even if they want to ...

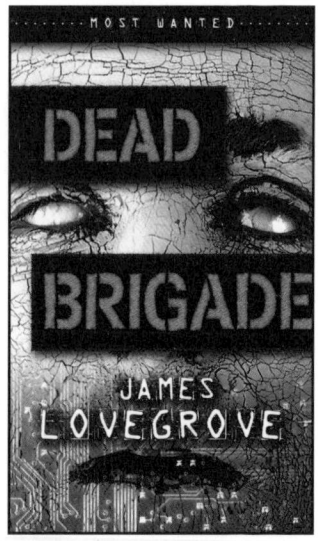

You can order these books directly from our website at www.barringtonstoke.co.uk

No More Victims
by
Natasha Cooper

Ben was picked on at school. Now he's dead – stabbed in the street, and left to bleed to death.
The police are hunting the killer. Candy thinks she knows who did it, and she wants him sent down.
But what if Candy's wrong?

Kill Clock
by
Allan Guthrie

The kill clock is ticking ... Pearce's ex-girlfriend is back. She needs twenty grand before midnight. Or she's dead. She doesn't have the money. Nor does Pearce. And time's running out. Fast ...

You can order these books directly from our website at
www.barringtonstoke.co.uk